For my mother, Helen Ruth Elliott,
who told her version of this story to her eight
children every Christmas Eve for many years L.S.

For my mum and dad A.W.

Text copyright © 2000 Linda Schlafer
Illustrations copyright © 2000 Anne Wilson
This edition copyright © 2000 Lion Publishing

The moral rights of the author and illustrator
have been asserted

Published by
Lion Publishing plc
Sandy Lane West, Oxford, England
www.lion-publishing.co.uk
ISBN 0 7459 4432 9

First edition 2000
10 9 8 7 6 5 4 3 2 1 0

A catalogue record for this book is available
from the British Library

Typeset in 17/25 Lapidary 333 BT
Printed and bound in Singapore

A Gift for the Christ Child

A Christmas Folktale

Linda Schlafer
Illustrated by Anne Wilson

High up in the mountains of a small country not far from here lived two young boys with their mother and grandfather. Around their hut was a modest clearing, covered now by a thin layer of snow through which a shrivelled cornstalk showed here and there. The wind cut through the woods, swooped across the clearing, and played ring-a-ring-a-roses around the little house.

Inside, the mother put another log on the fire, tucked a blanket more firmly about the grandfather's knees, and put the kettle on the hearthstones to boil. She set herself to weaving, glancing now and then to watch the boys, who were helping the grandfather shell corn. A small kitten also watched, pouncing on any stray kernel which slipped to the earth floor. The grandfather was telling a story as they worked.

From the valley far below came the faint sound of the church bell tolling the hour. The kettle hummed and the mother rose to make coffee. When it was ready and the grandfather's tale had ended, the mother spoke. 'Someone must go to the valley this year to carry our gift for the Christ Child,' she said.

The grandfather sighed a deep sigh and looked regretfully at his legs, withered as winter cornstalks. 'Daughter, I cannot go,' he said. 'But someone must carry our gift to the Christ Child.'

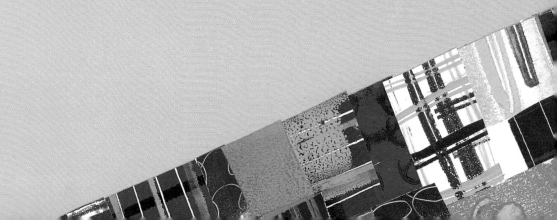

'I can do it!' cried Older Brother eagerly. He stood up quickly and stretched to his tallest height. 'See how much I have grown since last year!'

The mother saw her elder son's arms and legs where his clothing no longer covered them. She looked at his face, still bronzed by the summer sun.

'Yes,' she said at last. 'Yes. You must go together, you and Little Brother. So rest well, my sons, for tomorrow is Christmas Eve and you must leave at first light.'

Before the sun rose, the brothers dressed in all their clothes, for warmth. Their mother handed them each a bundle of food, and placed in Older Brother's palm the two copper coins which she had hoarded.

The boys set out on their long journey. The road was as white as the surrounding countryside, for few travellers passed that way. At first they went silently. In the eerie half-light their hearts feared to awaken the slumbering shapes which lay about them.

Then the sun rose and brightened the day. They shared some food, and Little Brother tried to imitate Older Brother's tuneful whistling as they made their way.

After a while they grew tired. And so, to cheer them, Older Brother recounted the purpose of their journey.

The sun rose to its height and then, once again, the shadows began to lengthen. The two boys were buffeted by sharp gusts of wind as heavy clouds gathered overhead. Older Brother took Little Brother's hand, and encouraged him with thoughts of the journey's end. Finally the town lay before them, and here and there a lantern shone against the approaching night. The brothers quickened their steps, eager now to reach their destination.

But a low moan surprised them. They stopped, dismayed. Surely it was just the wind they had heard! No, there it was again. 'Oh, let's run, let's run,' whimpered Little Brother, pulling on Older Brother's sleeve. But Older Brother had already turned and bent over a dark shape by the roadside. It was an old woman who had fallen and was unable to rise.

'Oh, come on, come on!' cried Little Brother. 'We'll never make it if we don't go on right now, and we must carry our gift to the Christ Child.'

Older Brother thought of the warm, brightly lit church. He thought of his mother's tales of rich men's clothes and beautiful music from the choir. He took a step to go with Little Brother, but the old woman cried again. He gave a quick shudder, knowing what he must do. He took the coins from his pocket and laid them in Little Brother's hand.

'She will die if we leave her,' he said. 'Go on alone now, in haste. First send help, then carry our gift to the Christ Child.'

Mournfully, Little Brother took the gift. 'Go on now, quickly,' urged Older Brother, and Little Brother began to run.

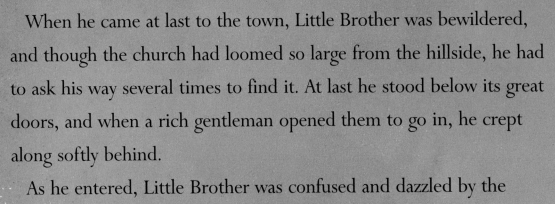

When he came at last to the town, Little Brother was bewildered, and though the church had loomed so large from the hillside, he had to ask his way several times to find it. At last he stood below its great doors, and when a rich gentleman opened them to go in, he crept along softly behind.

As he entered, Little Brother was confused and dazzled by the brilliance which lay about him. Warmth lulled his weary limbs and sleep came over him. But as his eyes closed, he pictured Older Brother on the dark hillside, and so with difficulty he roused himself.

All of the people who came and went seemed much too important to be troubled by such a poor, small child. Yet Little Brother knew he must find help, and he tugged timidly at the coat of a man who stood about. The man shrugged him off impatiently. Disappointed, Little Brother tried another person, and then yet another. Finally, a man who looked poorer than the rest bent his head down kindly to see what he would say.

When he had heard the boy's tale, the man motioned to a friend and went out quickly into the cold, dark night.

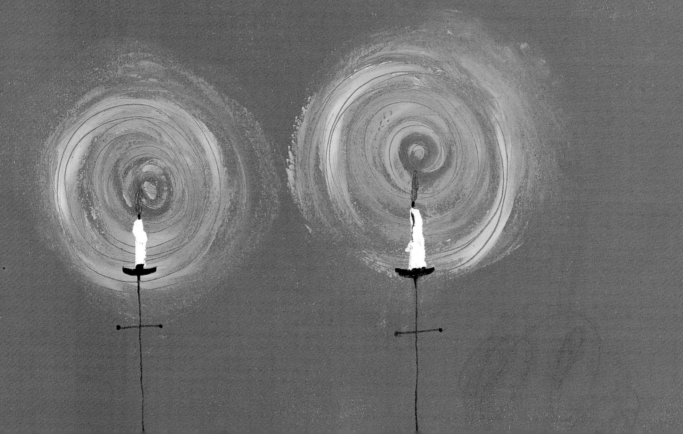

Then Little Brother remembered his gift, and he quietly slipped into a seat among the rich people gathered there. There was singing, and the little boy wondered if the angels themselves made music sweeter than that choir. He stared at the great rows of candles and the richly broidered tapestries in that fine church.

The time came for the gifts to be carried to the altar. One by one, the people rose to present their gifts, and everyone strained to see each marvellous offering. One man brought a bag which glittered with shining gold pieces. A woman cast down her rich furs. Another presented a casket of jewels.

Little Brother grew fearful of carrying his poor gift to the Christ Child amongst such splendour. Surely he will be offended by such a mean offering, the boy thought, and he held back until last. But then he remembered his mother and his grandfather high on the mountain, whose gift he carried. And he thought of Older Brother who could not be there as he had wished, to carry the gift himself. With new determination he went from his seat to lay his gift by the altar.

And then… and then the church bells began to play. Softly and
sweetly they began, then loud and wild and clear they rang for the whole
world to hear. The people in the church cried out in amazement. They
all knew the ancient legend that an angel would ring the chimes when a
gift had been given that was worthy of the Christ Child. Yet not one of
them could remember when the wonderful tunes had last been heard.

Up on the hillside, the mother smiled at the sweet sound. The
grandfather forgot his shrivelled limbs as the glorious peals echoed
in his heart, and the kitten danced for joy.

Along the dark, cold road where the poor man was carrying the old
woman and Older Brother trudged wearily through the snow, the music
enfolded them and lifted their spirits.

And the people of the church wondered what great gift this should be, to move the angel of the bells after so long a time. Every eye turned towards the altar to see what had been laid by it. But they never knew, for all they could see was a ragged urchin, curled up in the straw beside the cradle of the Christ Child. And the child stirred in his sleep and smiled as the music of the angel played in his dreams.